1-2-3
Va-Va-Vroom!
A Counting Book

by **Sarah Lynn**   illustrated by **Daniel Griffo**

Amazon Children's Publishing

Amazon Publishing
Attn: Amazon Children's Books
P.O. Box 400818
Las Vegas, NV 89149
www.amazon.com/amazonchildrenspublishing

Library of Congress Cataloging-in-Publication Data
Lynn, Sarah, 1975-
1-2-3 va-va-vroom! / by Sarah Lynn ; illustrated by Daniel Griffo. — 1st
Marshall Cavendish ed.
p. cm.
Summary: Playing with toy cars, three children find themselves flying
around a racetrack vying for first place.
ISBN 978-0-7614-6162-3 (hardcover) — ISBN 978-0-7614-6163-0
(ebook) [1. Toys—Fiction. 2. Automobiles—Fiction. 3. Racing—Fiction.
4. Play—Fiction. 5. Imagination—Fiction.] I. Griffo, Daniel, ill. II. Title.
III. Title: One-two-three va-va-vroom!
PZ7.L995252Aa 2012   [E]—dc23   2011036696

The illustrations are rendered in Adobe Photoshop.
Book design by Vera Soki
Editor: Marilyn Brigham

Printed in China (W)
First edition
10 9 8 7 6 5 4 3 2 1

For my three little men, Benjamin, Noah, and Jacob
—S. L.

For my beloved son Benjamin
—D. G.

Lap One!
Checkered flag.
Seatbelt strapped!
Helmet snapped!
Screeching down the lane!

Va-va-vroom!

Lap Two!
Crouch down low.
Give it gas.
Try to pass,
zooming for the lead!

Va-va-vroom!

Lap Four!
Hard to steer.
Tire squeals!
Spinning wheels!
Flipping! Twisting! Land!

Va-va-vroom!

Lap Five!
Round-the-loop,
splash through mud.
Pop! Thud—thud.
Limping to the pit.
Va-va-vroom!

Lap Six!
Fill 'er up.
Engines whir.
Crowd's a blur.
Racing off again!

LAP 6

Va-va-vroom!

Lap Seven!
Speed it up.
Swooshing flags,
tailpipe drags,
sparking past the crowd!

Va-va-vroom!

LAP
7

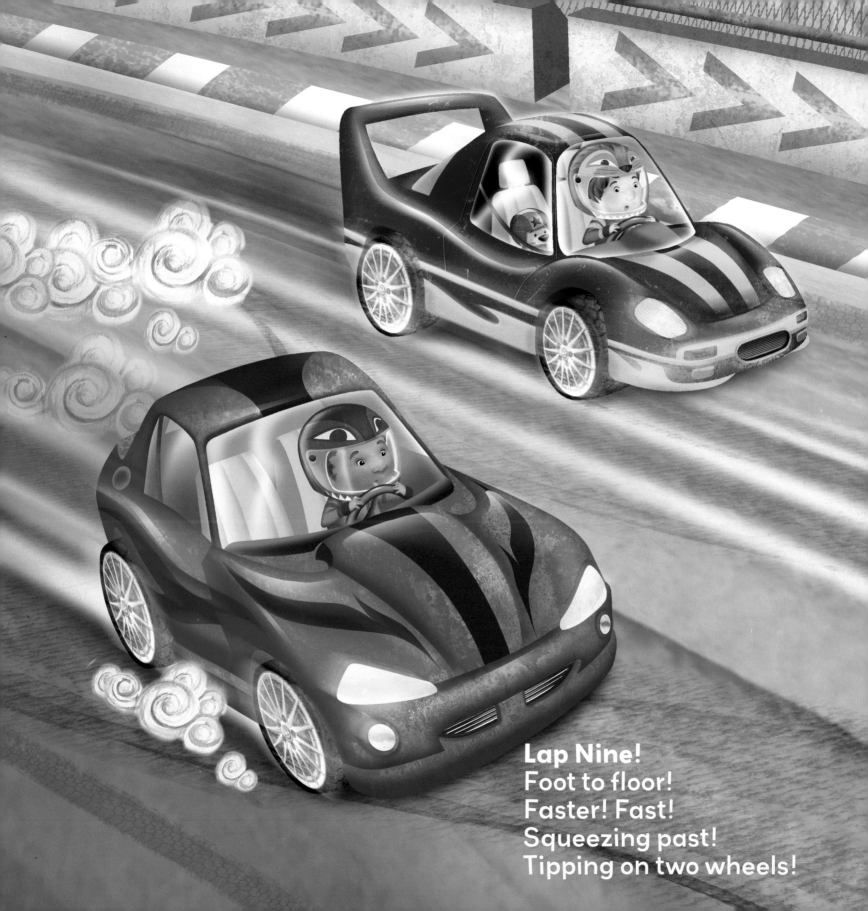

Lap Nine!
Foot to floor!
Faster! Fast!
Squeezing past!
Tipping on two wheels!

Lap Ten!
Hear the crowd
cheer and clap.
Final lap!
Blasting past the line.

Va-va-vroom!

Slow it down.
Great big grin.
Friends rush in.
Waving from up high.

Ba-ba-boom!

Ba-ba-boom!

Grape snow cones!
Kettle corn!
Sound the horn!
Showing off the prize!

Celebrate!
Stand up proud.
Cheer out loud.
Revving up again!

Va-va-vroom!